My Pet

GUINEA PIG

Kate Petty

Stargazer Books

The guinea pig

Guinea pigs are sometimes called cavies. Wild cavies were first found in South America. They belong to the same big family of animals as hamsters and squirrels.

Guinea pigs have been kept as pets for about 400 years. They make very good pets for children because they are gentle and easy to tame. They usually live for about five years.

Pretty guinea pigs, like this smooth-haired one, can be bought from most pet stores.

Wild cavies probably looked like this Golden Agouti guinea pig. ▶

All sorts of guinea pigs

What sort of guinea pig would you choose? One with smooth hair or one with rough hair growing in little rosettes?

Some guinea pigs have very long, silky hair that covers their faces so that you can't tell which end is which! There are many different colored guinea pigs. Some of the light-colored ones have pink eyes.

Smooth-haired guinea pig

Three different sorts of coats

Peruvian guinea pig

Abyssinian (rosette) guinea pig

A Tortoiseshell Peruvian is usually only available from a breeder. ▶

Looking at a guinea pig

Guinea pigs are prettier than many of their rodent cousins. As with all rodents, their teeth are made for gnawing. The front teeth, called incisors, never stop growing. Guinea pigs need hard food to wear them down.

A full-grown guinea pig is 8-10 inches (20–25 cm) long. It has short ears, short legs, and no tail. Healthy guinea pigs have bright eyes and glossy hair.

The guinea pig has long front teeth for gnawing.

All guinea pigs have the same smooth, rounded shape, like this Gray Agouti. ▶

On the move

Guinea pigs scamper around quickly on their short legs, but they cannot jump or climb. Guinea pigs need as much space as possible to run around in. If they don't have enough exercise they can become fat.

Guinea pigs in a run need to be protected from other animals. The run should be covered on all sides, including underneath, with wire netting.

A run like this can be moved every few days to provide fresh grass for the guinea pigs.

Guinea pigs have four toes on their front feet but only three on their back feet. ▶

Eating

Wild cavies spend their lives grazing on the grasslands. Pet guinea pigs spend a lot of time eating, too. They need to be fed twice a day.

Guinea pigs must have a mixture of dry grains and fresh food. Root vegetables, like carrots, and leaves, such as lettuce and dandelion, keep a guinea pig healthy. It also needs plenty of water to drink.

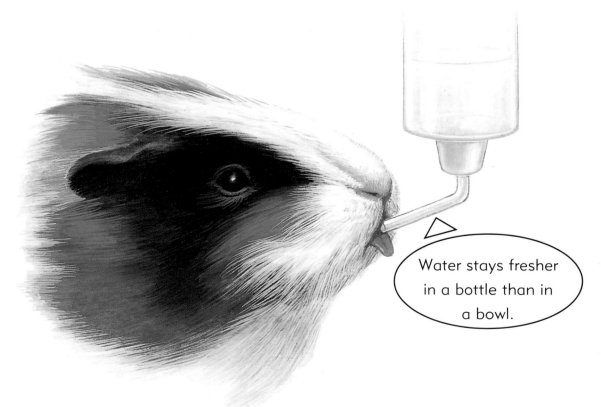

Water stays fresher in a bottle than in a bowl.

A carrot helps to wear down the incisors, in addition to providing vitamins. ▶

Sociable guinea pigs

In the wild, guinea pigs live in large groups. One living alone in captivity can get lonely. Several female guinea pigs will live together happily, but two boars (males) in the same cage will almost certainly fight.

A guinea pig will willingly share its cage with a rabbit, but if it has to live alone it will need lots of attention from its owner to keep it happy.

Guinea pigs are naturally timid creatures.

Guinea pig friends often huddle together. ▶

Chatterboxes

Guinea pigs are friendly little creatures. Once they are used to people they can become very tame. They soon learn when it is feeding time and will run around squeaking with excitement.

Guinea pigs are very chatty. They make a whole range of sounds, from noisy squeaks to a variety of contented grunts and chirrups.

Guinea pigs will often take food from your hand.

This guinea pig is looking to see if its next meal is on the way. ▶

Newborn guinea pigs

Most rodents are pregnant for 21 days and their babies are born blind, hairless, and helpless. Guinea pigs are pregnant for 68 days. Newborn guinea pigs have open eyes, hair, and all their teeth.

The mother usually has two to four babies—and occasionally six. She can only feed two at a time.

The babies feed from their mother for the first three weeks of their lives.

This guinea pig is only a few minutes old, but it will soon be on its feet. ▶

Growing up

A newborn guinea pig can run around an hour after it is born. It weighs about 3 ounces (85 grams). By the time it is fully grown—at about six months—it will be ten times that weight.

When they are eight weeks old, pet guinea pigs can go to new homes and can even start having babies of their own.

newborn
3 in (8 cm)

1 year
8-10 in (20-25 cm)

8-10 weeks
5-6 in (13-16 cm)

An Abyssinian mother with her babies ▶

Handle with care

Guinea pigs hardly ever bite or scratch. Be very careful not to drop a guinea pig because it can be badly hurt by a fall. Hold it firmly when you pick it up.

Support the weight of its hindquarters with one hand and grasp it around the shoulders with the other. It will respond to being stroked with little chattering noises.

The correct way to pick up a guinea pig

An Abyssinian's rosettes can be carefully groomed with a toothbrush. ▶

Know your guinea pigs

This chart will help you to recognize some of the different breeds of guinea pigs. A special guinea pig show is the best place to see them.

Guinea pigs vary in hair type and color. Breeders are always trying to find new variations. A full-grown guinea pig is about the same size as a man's shoe.

Roan Abyssinian

Short-haired Self Black

Tricolor Sheltie

Rough-haired
Tortoiseshell and
White

Golden
Agouti

Peruvian

Tortoiseshell
and White

23

Index

©Aladdin Books Ltd 2006

Produced by
Aladdin Books Ltd

First published in the
United States in 2006 by
Stargazer Books
c/o The Creative Company
123 South Broad Street
P.O. Box 227
Mankato, Minnesota 56002

Designer: Pete Bennett – PBD
Editor: Rebecca Pash
Illustrator: George Thompson
Picture Research: Cee Weston-Baker

Printed in Malaysia

All rights reserved

Photographic credits:
Cover: PBD; pages 19 & 21: Zefa; pages 3, 5
7, 9, 11, 13 & 17: Bruce Coleman Ltd; page
15: Sally Anne Thompson/Animal Photograph

Library of Congress Cataloging-in-Publication Data

Petty, Kate.
    Guinea pig / by Kate Petty.
        p. cm. -- (My pet)
    ISBN 1-59604-029-7
        1. Guinea pigs as pets--Juvenlle literature
    I. Title.

SF459.G9P468 2005
636.935'92--dc22
                                        2004060731